ROUND TRIP
ANN JONAS

P9-CWD-866

GREENWILLOW BOOKS

An Imprint of HarperCollinsPublishers

Round Trip
Copyright © 1983 by Ann Jonas. All rights
reserved. Manufactured in China.
For information address HarperCollins Children's
Books, a division of HarperCollins Publishers,
195 Broadway, New York, NY 10007.
www.harperchildrens.com

Library of Congress Cataloging in
Publication Data
Jonas, Ann. Round trip.
"Greenwillow Books."
Summary: Black and white illustrations and
text record the sights on a day trip to the city
and back home again to the country.
[1. Cities and towns—Fiction.
2. Country life—Fiction.]
I. Title.
PZ7.J664Ro 1983   [E]   82-12026
ISBN 0-688-01772-X (trade)
ISBN 0-688-01781-9 (lib. bdg.)
ISBN 0-688-09986-6 (pbk.)

First Edition
16 17 18 19 20 SCP 20 19 18 17

For Don Nina Amy

We started out as soon as it was light.

Our neighborhood was quiet, the houses dark.
The sun shone on the pond.

and soon saw our moonlit street.

Town was empty,
the stores still closed.

We took the tunnel under the river,

We passed a small farm in the valley,

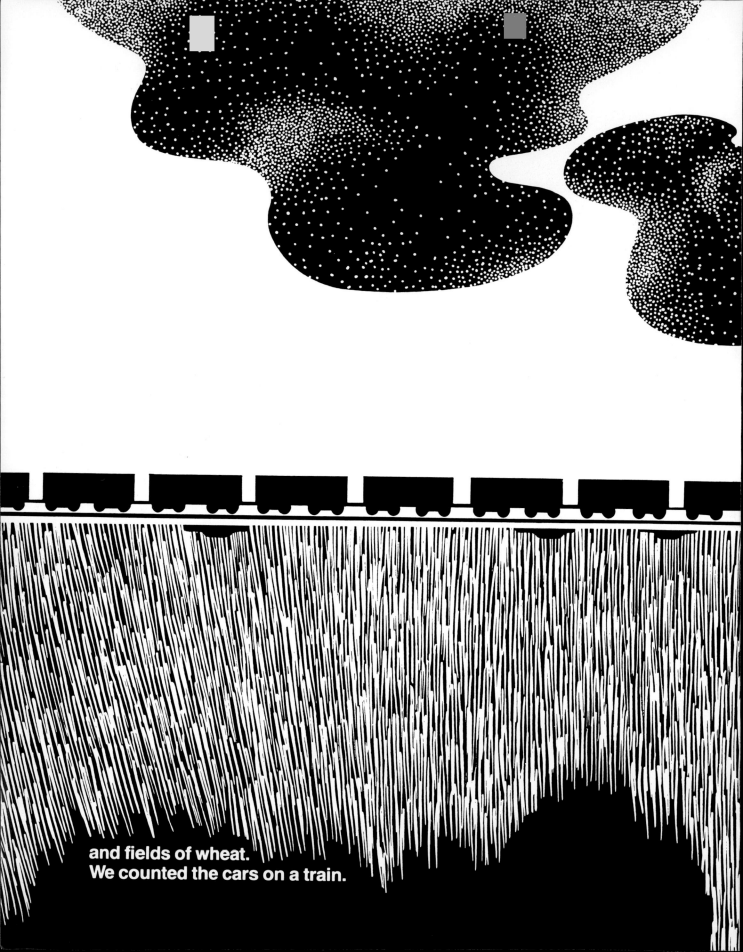

and fields of wheat.
We counted the cars on a train.

It rained hard
and puddles formed.

The road wound through the mountains.
Trails led into the woods.

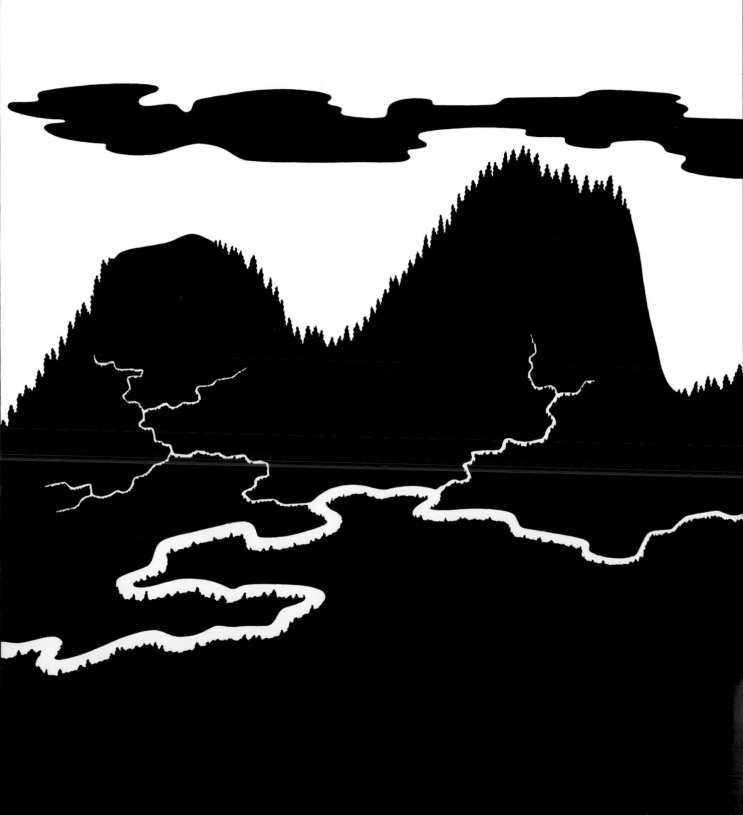

Lightning flashed across the sky.

On the highway,
we headed for the coast.

We went under an expressway.

The water was rough, the waves high,

As the smoke from the fireworks drifted away
and the birds resettled in the trees, we drove on.

We followed the shore past marshy inlets
and summer cottages.

We saw fireworks and stopped to watch.

Then we saw the city.

We looked back. Searchlights pierced the sky.

We crossed a bridge,

In the country, telephone poles lined the road.

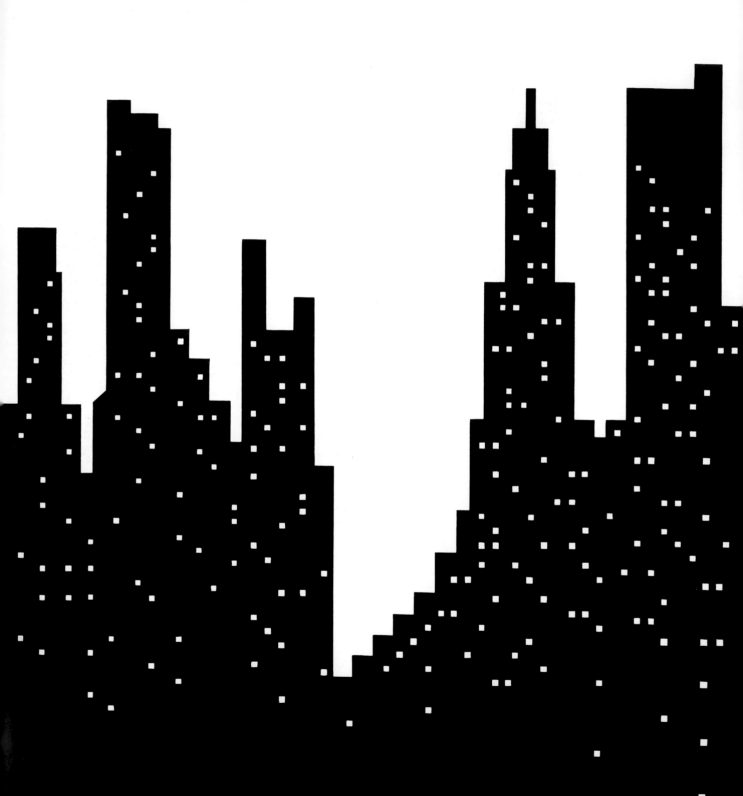

and we were there

We left the shining, starlit city.

After parking the car, we rode the subway.

and picked up our car from the garage.

Then we went to a movie.

and to the top of the tallest building.
We looked down.

Back on the street,
we looked up at where we had been.

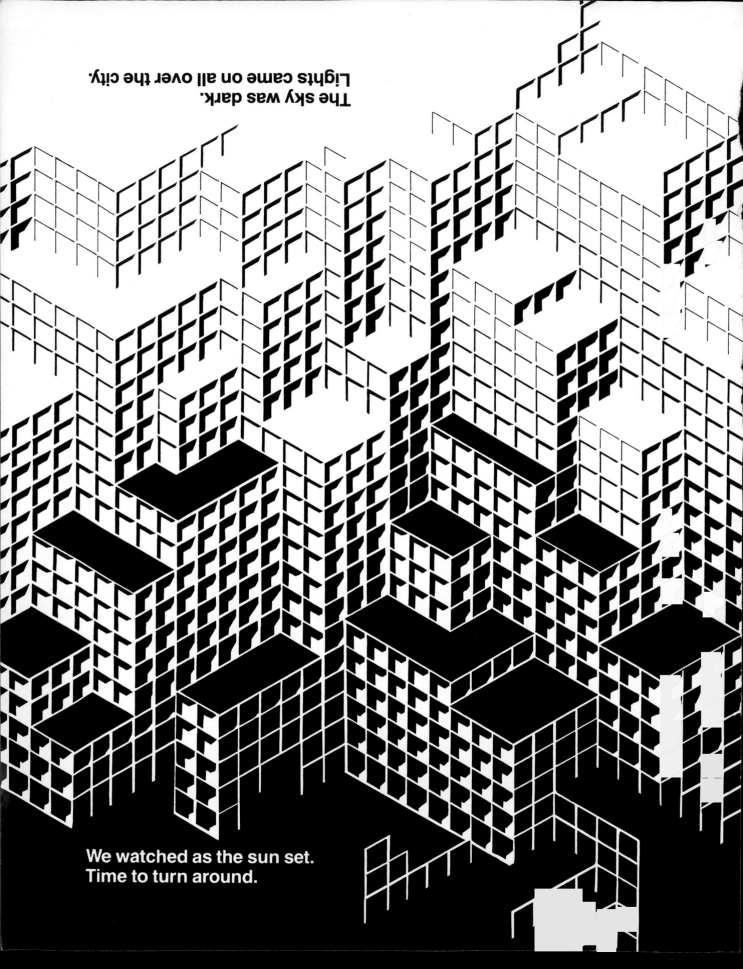

The sky was dark.
Lights came on all over the city.

We watched as the sun set.
Time to turn around.